WOMEN OF GROOM

YOU ONLY GET TO KNOW HER IN THE ASS.

MARIA VALLEETSY

COPYRIGHT © 2024

Maria Valleetsy

Copyright

The work, including its parts, is protected by copyright. Any use is not permitted without the consent of the publisher and the author. This applies in particular to electronic or other reproduction, translation, distribution and making available to the public.

Edited By:
Maria Valleetsy

First Printing Edition, 2024

Imprint: Independently published

Welcome to a journey into a world of passion, desire and discovery. In this book you will find a storie that delve deep into the fascinating world of BDSM and SM. It is a world in which
pleasure and pain unite, where dominance and devotion merge into a dance of the senses.
These storie not only bring us closer to physical acts, but above all to the deep emotions that arise between the protagonists.
arise between the protagonists. It is about trust, letting go of control, exploring one's own boundaries and liberation from social norms.
Dark sides may appear in the stories, but at their core they shine with the brightness of the human soul. They tell of
longings, of the search for fulfillment and of the power that lies in the intimacy of two people.

Author

In my real life, I am a sex therapist. It's not just professionally that I'm obsessed with sex.

In my free time, I travel around the country and enjoy visiting

Swingers clubs. Privately and professionally

I experience the hottest and hottest stories and sex confessions.

My patients and me

and my sex partners tell me the wildest smut, which I put on paper uncensored and pass on exactly

and pass them on. In addition to my passion for wild sex without taboos, I don't mince my words

mouth and let my acquaintances bluntly and in all horniness about their perverse sexual experiences.

experiences. In these books, I only write down what my sexual acquaintances and patients tell me.

and patients tell me. The names of the people have of course been changed.

WOMEN OF GROOM

YOU ONLY GET TO KNOW HER IN THE ASS.

WOMEN OF GROOM

We always had mixed feelings about Jennifer and Frank. Jennifer is Angie's best friend and so it was clear when she decided to marry Frank that my wife would be maid of honor. As befits good friends, Jenni also became Angie's maid of honor and we men got along.

There were mixed feelings because we both think Frank is a brutal asshole. In our opinion, you can see it on his face. He is shaved bald, his cold blue eyes are close together, and an often distant and imperious grin is hidden under his pointed nose.

He's really not a pretty man, but he's tall and strong, and what you should never forget is that he earns a lot of money.

We don't actually know anyone from Jenni's family who really likes Frank.

Although, I have to admit that Frank has qualities in two areas that suit me. He can tolerate alcohol and knows a thing or two about football. You can spend an evening with this while the women talk about the banal things in life.

It wasn't the first time Angie and I thought about why Jennifer married this guy. I mostly stopped at the money and assumed that he must be a good engraver who is definitely much more open and affectionate when there are two of them.

There are men who see it as weakness when they are affectionate and affectionate towards their wives in public. On the other hand, I barely knew

Jenni, only knew about a few stories that should have made me suspicious. "Well, women from the East," that's how I thought about my wife too.

Even if she were to leave me one day, I would always try to talk to a woman from East Germany, because Angie's predecessors from the old Federal Republic of Germany were never so free and open.

Be that as it may, we packed our things and drove from Munich towards Saxony. It was slipping well on the A9 and I was in a good mood anyway, as last night we had another one of those memorable fucks that should never end.

Angie probably thought the same and again her hand moved along my thigh to my fly. My cock immediately stiffened. There's nothing wrong with Angie's skills as a playmate.

She does a lot of the things I really like, and better yet, she enjoys doing them too.

With some reservations, of course, she doesn't always allow me to let her piss on me when I climb into her back entrance, she sometimes finds it funny and otherwise often just amusing. NS doesn't turn her on, even if she knows that my cock will immediately stand out. She finds restraints cool. If I blindfold her, her little one immediately starts dripping.

But if I grab her too hard, when she's lying spread-eagled and exposed in front of me, the lust will immediately go out the window. Torture is not for them and actually not for me either.

On the other hand, she does love getting her ass pounded when my cock is between her gorgeous thighs and I'm thrusting her into the sky.

Then she even encourages me not to make things difficult for her. She's like a wild animal and that's why we have the most fun fucking, banging like rabbits with no regard for tomorrow.

The A93 is free to Regensburg. Nowadays I also touch her heavy breasts from time to time. I love her tits so much that she sometimes jokes that I wouldn't have married her without the milk swings. Of course that's nonsense, even if I like it more buxom.

We're starting to talk about Jennifer and Frank again. Jenni turned 30 last week, making her two years older than Angie.

She's not really pretty, but she has that certain something. The last time we were there, she was sitting at the table at breakfast wearing only a nightgown. It was clear she wasn't wearing anything underneath and then she put both feet on the kitchen chair, flashing her pussy for a moment.

Shaved, it was logical, just like Angie. But I also knew that without seeing it. The two of them shaved their pubic mounds bald when they were teenagers.

Frank freaked out, immediately sent her to the bedroom and ordered her to put some clothes on. No joke, he ordered her to do it in front of more or less strangers, and she quickly scurried into the marriage chamber and put something on.

It wasn't anything bad or special for both girls to show themselves. They had known nudism since childhood and thought nothing of it.

Our curtains are always open at home when we walk around the apartment naked. Who would ignore us? On the contrary, it's much hotter in summer when you're fucking and the windows are open.

Everyone can hear how well my wife is doing. At least it doesn't hurt my self-confidence, on the contrary and it turns my sweetheart on quite a bit.

Angie once again thinks about how much she doesn't like this guy. As usual, I play the mediator. Tell her that it's her best friend and she must have had something in mind at the wedding. They had known each other for a few days beforehand.

Then the story comes back that some people change after they have what they wanted and the usual complaining continues all the way to Plauen.

I stopped paying too much attention to strangers' bed stories a long time ago. Angie can sprawl over it for hours. It would be much better if it were spread out on the hood of a remote forest path in Upper Franconia right now.

Of course nothing happens when I ask her because she doesn't want my juice dripping out of her naked woman for the rest of the trip. You wish for a little spontaneity and what do you get? Shaggy on the radio and my balls bounce unsatisfied to the beat of the bass.

After finally arriving after five hours, we first have a beer. In that respect, Frank is really the perfect host and knows what we need after a long and unsatisfactory journey. Of course he doesn't offer the women anything to drink. I find myself not really bothered by it at all, let alone particularly noticing it right now.

He cooks and loves cooking. So we're standing in the somewhat dingy kitchen, the women are taking a long look at the new living room. It doesn't take long before we end up on the only topic on which I can get along with every person in the world, even if they are the worst: football.

Today I also prepared a little regionally, and when the first beer was gone, he sent Jenni to the cellar to get the beer.

I can hardly light my next cigarette so quickly and there is another beer in front of me.

"Let Harald open the bottle himself!" Frank shouts at his little one.

"Where is the opener? Frank, where did you put that?"

Jenni's voice trembles slightly.

"Let it go," I say. "I'll take the lighter!"

"You close the beer bottle. Jennifer does that!"

His cold eyes sparkled.

"Great," I thought, "then we would be ready for my wife to scratch Frank's eyes out."

In fact, it only takes a few moments and Angie is standing in the kitchen with her head very red. "Let's go for a walk," Jenni says to my wife,

"I'm sure the men can handle themselves here too," and smiles at me as she puts a fresh pilsner in front of me. Frank grins and toasts me like a winner. The women head outside and Frank checks the pots.

"I can open my own beer," I say. "Sure you can, but you're not at home here and it's Jennie's job to look after the guests. It's embarrassing enough what the kitchen looks like again.

I work 11 hours every day and when I come home there isn't even anything hot on the table." He tried the sauce. "I thought you liked cooking?" "Sure," Frank replies, "but not internally and if I'm going to bring in the money, I expect a little in return."

When is Jennifer going back to work?" I ask. "Not at all. What I earn is enough for both of us. Cheers, Harald"

Pushed and betrayed myself. Mr. Enlightened, who always rambles on about how important it is that both of them work, seems to cope quite well when others don't.

Now would be exactly the right time to say something. Instead, I have Frank's new computer explained to me and listen intently to the big monologue about his plan for success.

Shortly before five the women come back. The walk seems to have been good. Both girls appear laughing and trusting. Frank has already changed his clothes and I feel stupid again because he's strutting around the apartment in a suit and tie.

Jennie approaches Frank and kisses him deeply. It's obvious that he grabs her ass firmly, which is actually from good parents, a bit expansive but not really wide, with visibly firm and well-trained flesh.

I find myself seeing Jennie in the inferior role and immediately viewing her in a more derogatory way than I normally think of women.

Spurred on by the two of them, Angie also comes to me, kisses me as well and runs her hand under my shirt and briefly brushes my right nipple. In any case, there's no question about who's wearing the pants here, birthday or not.

And so it's no wonder that after the rest of the guests have arrived, Jennifer is constantly running and serving, giving Frank the Great Gatsby at the head of the table.

His nagging laugh echoes through the room again and again, while the other guests - some disturbed, some politely deflecting attention - take part in the conversation.

Angie pulls me into the kitchen for a cigarette. "Look at this, this isn't normal. Jennie can't calm down. This is their celebration! And the bag just sits at the table and can be served!"

Angie is beside herself. "Maybe she likes it that way," I say. "Like something like that? To serve your guy?" Angie's question sounds contemptuous. "Yes," I reply. "You are crazy. "I've known Jennie since I was 14," says Angie indignantly.

"I find a few things strange,"

I murmur, "like the fact that she doesn't want to go to work." "Because he won't let her," Angie hisses, or do you think the studies should be for free?" "Maybe..."

Jennifer's mother comes into the kitchen smiling tiredly. Frank's behavior clearly bothers her.

"Well, what's life like in Munich?" "Nice Rosie, we're getting along just fine," I hear Angie say. "Listen," she says, "Frank is completely different,

I don't even know what's going on with him today," she smiles around for help. "It's okay," says my wife,

"Will you have a Baileys with me too?"

"No, Dad and I are just leaving. I just wanted to say a quick goodbye."

The evening quickly dissipated. Before 11 p.m. everyone except us who sleep here had disappeared. People said goodbye politely and usually without any particular interest.

Angie and I are standing in the kitchen. "Are you still going home?" she asked. "To Munich? Only if the chauffeur is called Jägermeister.

Stop it, I'm pretty drunk and for you it's at least the tenth champagne." "I have no idea. But I don't want to stay here." and cuddles up to my chest like a cat and does the "You're the best man in the world because you do everything for me" number. "Let's go into the room again. It's so quiet there, maybe he's already eaten her."

Now even my wife laughs, despite the impossible evening. It's only three or four steps to the living room. I get the impression that with the last step I will enter a new world.

Jenni sits at the foot of the chair with both knees drawn up and her thighs turned to the side. Supporting yourself with your hands, your posture can deliberately be considered comfortable. Frank sits in an armchair with his legs apart, a cognac snifter in his hand and strokes her hair.

"Didn't my Jennie do well this evening?" he asks.

Once again, as I sit down, I notice that he only ever looks at me and only talks to me, even though Angie is also there. "Come on, snail," he says, "pour Harald a cognac too. But not the cheap stuff for the other proles."

Jennie jumps up so quickly that she almost falls over. Frank grabs her by the blouse, where – of course – one of the buttons on the front comes off. But that leaves Frank cold and Jennie doesn't bother to fix the blouse, which had now lost a button right between her tits. In general,

I now notice that there are candles burning in every corner and, in contrast to the rest of the evening, there is some decent music playing, Victor Laszlo. The mood has changed.

Jennie pours me plenty. "Cheers Frank!" I say and ignore Angie's look, which I'll probably have to deal with tomorrow.

But what can you say: the girl does everything the guy orders.

I mean, it's weird and somehow exactly what's making me a little horny right now. That's why I quickly look over the edge of the snifter at my wife, knowing what pleasure she can give me. Presto, the cock is heated up again and to make matters worse, my bent over sits on my lap. Thank you very much. And then I say something that I had on my lips hours before and that now bubbles out, asked or unasked.

"Tell me, Frank," I think for a moment, "isn't the way you chase Jennie around a bit too much?" I go one step further. "She's your wife and has a little more…" "A little more what?" grins Frank. "Deserves a little more tenderness," I soften. "Jennifer," Frank croons, "come to me."

That wasn't actually necessary, as she knelt at his feet again and was now looking at him completely in love.

"Right to me!"

that was louder. One last look at Angie and she sits down between his thighs, nestles her head on the inside of his right thigh and clearly strokes his lap with her left hand, even squeezing every now and then when she feels something firm under her hand.

I unconsciously lick my lips. I mean, and I repeat myself, she's not particularly pretty, but that devotion. Different, completely different from my home. I looked at Angie.

The same. One hundred percent, I know her, know her far too well. She is interested, excited about what is happening here.

He leans forward. Puts his lips on her right ear, looks up at us, "Am I treating you badly?" No, love." it came out of her mouth as if it were a matter of course. That wasn't an act.

"Are you dissatisfied, do you want me to change?"

Frank grins over her head at me. "Never lover, please Angie, don't you understand?" She had turned away from him and was looking into the eyes of her maid of honor.

Only now does Angie begin to understand what she had always seen. I can really see her mind racing through Jennifer's relationships , past all of her lovers, to what they have in common. "Are you his slave ?

Is that your idea of love?" my wife was curious about the answer. "You don't understand, snail," said Jennifer. "But she understands, she understands really well," says Frank, standing up by pushing his wife aside with his right knee.

Frank's eyes stare at me as he approaches Angie, and when he naturally pinches her right breast and then caresses her cheek, he shows me how well my wife understands.

Angie is indignant and shouts at him, shouting something about pigs and at the same time clinging to his finger, which forces itself demandingly between her thighs.

I'm paralyzed. At Frank's behest, Jennie starts working on my fly. Her hands have no trouble opening the zipper.

My cock is hard. But he was already that way before this scene. Frank grabs Angie's neck with one hand and squeezes. He wants her to look at him and she does so with wide, indignant eyes.

"What do you want cunt, what do you want" his other hand disappears under her sweater, his lips are pressed together from the exhausting fight with her.

I suspect what the cunt wants, but I can hardly think about it because my cock slides so wonderfully in and out between my wife's maid of honor's lips.

I'm not doing anything. I let everything happen as it comes and it doesn't take a minute and Jennie swallows while Frank, now grabbing my wife by the neck, forces me to watch.

Jennie swallows extensively and takes what comes out between her cock and lips with her finger and then licks it off. "Later, if you can give yourself more time, we'll try again later." Her smile is stunningly submissive . There is no woman sitting here, a pleasure maid, a magnificent woman is sitting here.

Angie pushes Frank aside with all her strength, breaks free from his grip, gives me a lifelong slap right in the face and disappears into the bedroom. Jennie follows her, which Frank allows with a nod.

"My little one sucks well, doesn't she?"

"Tell me, are you stupid?

How am I supposed to straighten this out!" I'm
fucking pissed." my voice vibrates. "I especially like
the spot when she just pampers you with her
tongue shortly before you inject. You know, just
the tongue, very tenderly, lashing the underside of
your glans, hot isn't it?" Frank reaches for the
cognac bottle again.

"Stop getting me drunk or you'll get to know me."

"Don't act like the strong man here. Who injected
my wife in the face, you or me." "You're not doing
it right!" I get up from the chair and want to go
into the bedroom to my wife, my beloved Angie,
who is now probably crying between the pillows.

"Harald! Stay here and drink. Finish your cognac.
Jennie is different, don't you understand that?"
"Oh and that's why everyone has to be different," I
whine. "Not everyone, but you, after all Angie is
our maid of honor.

Or do you think we're pulling this number because
of you? It doesn't matter whether the in-laws
understand that. Your other boring friends?

I can also fuck the vacuum cleaner. But Angie is important to Jennie and if I'm honest, with you I can even imagine that I'll let you have a real go at Jennie. I like you." "And you probably like my wife too!"

"Angie? "If it's even half as good as Jennie says, you must be really happy," Frank grins. "Harald, come on, two pussies, both wet and horny, what more do you want?" Frank toasts me.

"The difference is that mine is packing her suitcases forever." "Now stay calm, let Jennie do it. She's a really sensitive girl, she's licked Angie to her first climax as we speak."

I look over at Frank in disbelief at what I'm hearing. "Don't say you don't know that. You don't know that? Hammer. But do you already know what underwear your wife wears? None, right?" "Pour a glass," I hold out my glass, "now go ahead and pour a glass."

"I like you better that way and now take off those damn clothes. The girls are really getting it tonight."

"If you hit my wife or torture her in any other way, I'll knock the place down for you," is what I wanted to at least make clear. "Just watch what I do. You'll see that violence has its limits, and I'll tell you one thing, I have never and will never punish Jennifer against her will." and he pours himself and me another drink.

"Tell me, Jennifer doesn't mind if you rule over her in front of everyone here?" "On the contrary, it makes her horny and when I sometimes really put her over my knee after an evening like this, she becomes the cuddliest kitten ever .

But think further, Jennie doesn't mind if I fuck your wife. She even wishes that. If you say no, then no. Otherwise, I'll make it supple today." "And I'll do it with Jennie?" "As often and whenever you want, as long as I decide.

Otherwise you can forget it. If my wife isn't being used dominantly , you can put two tablespoons of lubricant in her pussy and nothing will happen." In just a few simple steps I'm naked and show off my masculinity, which is quite impressive: my tattoos, my muscles, not least my cock.

Gotcha! Here I stand, I can't help it. When Frank grabs my cock, I think I'm in the wrong movie and I let him do it anyway. In the end it only lasts a short time and he also gets up and undresses.

"Hefty too, that sack," I think. No tattoos, but an equally shaved cock. He goes over to the cabinet and takes out a belt. It has a few loops. Apparently some accessories can be attached to it.

There is a whip in the same drawer . Hanging around his neck, it dangles down to his feet. I'm excited to see what will happen when Angie's gorgeous ass gets to know the part.

Frank can drink, knows a thing or two about football and is currently fulfilling my biggest dream, fucking around until the doctor leaves, banging like an animal and then driving home with his wife and being happy together.

Angie and Jennifer disappeared into the bedroom. As we talked, one woman told the other how she really met Frank. This was something that was never supposed to happen and yet it was in a swingers club in Hesse.

Both then said goodbye to their relationships and ended up happily back in Saxony. "Count it," Jennie said as she lowered her pants. The welts are obvious.

Angie didn't have to count, she immediately saw that there were nine of them, stretched across her best friend's ass, which was once very red, but not split open and is now almost completely healed.

"Frank isn't always like that, sometimes I have to encourage him. Three days ago he came home at nine and I hadn't made dinner. That really hurt. But afterwards he fucked me like a bull, first dry in the ass and then in the pussy.

Normal doesn't work for me anymore. He can't get it up and I'm so dry, oh well. But when he has me under his thumb!" Jennie smiles dreamily and strokes Angie's cheek and lips with her finger.

"You gave my husband a blowjob!" Angie backs away from the finger. "There was no other way. Otherwise we wouldn't be lying here. Evil? I've found your husband hot ever since he danced with me at the wedding. So determined."

"Yes, he can dance well. And that's why you're blowing him?"

"Remember that time" and her hands began to unzip her pants. "Stop it Jennie, it's been so long."

"My pussy still tastes just as good, does yours?"

“Jennie, please don’t!”

Jennifer's hands have long since gone further than Angie's will. “You’re a pig,” Angie said. “You know that, snail, and now I’ve finally found the man who knows how to treat a pig like me.”

“You put up with all of this voluntarily?”

“That and more. But before I let strangers get to my holes, I want to try and see if my dearest, sweetest, little friend doesn't want to play with us."

"I can't do that," says Angie and had already pulled her jeans down to her knees. She doesn't wear panties anyway and she thinks that's totally dirty and thinks that it makes me strappy, which it always does.

“Your husband is already in the mood” and a finger wanders into Angie’s ass while the thumb circles on her bud. “And how is this supposed to continue?” Angie tried to free herself.

"We'll fuck the four of us, or we'll find others."

"Frank won't come into my pussy, you can forget that." "Let's see," Jennie devours her best friend's cunt, licking it from her thighs up into hers Delta between her legs, dancing over the bud, sucking the flesh, running her tongue out and in again and again and then reaching for the breasts, twirling the teats, really hurting Angie.

The juices are boiling in Angie. As before, she holds out her gift table and arches her pelvis forward. "I'll do it to you now, but only if Frank can fuck you. Can he fuck you?" Jennie asks with a dream of a pout. "No, never." Angie is still indignant but horny, so helplessly horny.

Jennifer reaches for the fat udders again, one hand goes under the bed and grabs clips on a chain.

She continues licking the pussy, pushes a finger up to the first member into the tight anus, has nothing left for Angie's fear as she fastens the clamps on the nipples - the small, oh-so-sensitive ones - "Snap, snap" where they belong and Then, almost at the moment of orgasm, he has first two, then three and now four fingers in Angie's ass.

"Frank can fuck you and I'll finish you" "No, never! Finish me off. Please finish me." Frank, fuck you in the ass with my fist in your cunt and I'll finish you." "No, not another man...no." The fingers rotated, the flesh twitched wildly.

"Frank rubs your ass off and bucks you like a boar."

"Snail, finish me, finish me, let me come." Angie is wild with lust. Her juices are flowing. Your synapses explode.

Electric shocks of hot fantasies pulsate through her brain, turning her head into cinema. The hand fills her, the clamps don't torture her, they become a part of her and when Jennifer starts to pull on the chain that connects the two nasty clamps:

"Frank is doing what?" "Frank is fucking me." Angie moans out of here.

"Where is Frank fucking you?"

"In the ass," she gasps, is about to burst, "Frank is fucking me really hot in the ass," she is about to, "long and persistent," one fist could bring her so much fulfillment, "in the aaaaaaaaaarsssssshhhh!"

Her arrival is also heard by the men who actually don't feel like dealing with Remy Martin anymore.

"You hear, Harald, I told you. Now it's a draw. A blow job for you and a lick through the honey pot for Angie."

I toast Frank with some relief. If Angie really got it well, then she's in a good mood now. Just wondering how she will react when she sees both of us guys sitting here naked. But somehow everything doesn't matter now. Of course I'll leave the further management to Frank, but that's a given. "Woman, come here," Frank calls through the apartment.

You quickly hear rustling in the bedroom, the door flies open and Jennifer takes small, quick steps into the living room, kneels in front of her husband, puts her hands behind her neck and arches her back. Her mediocre tits stand firm in the room with pointed nipples. Her ass must have taken some beating in the last few days, all in all a great sight.

But my little wife looks even hotter to me. Really worn out and disheveled, she comes out of the bedroom on weak legs and sinks onto the couch with wide thighs.

Her pussy is wide open and the lobes glisten wetly. The clamps and chain still hang on her heavy breasts. She doesn't mind that we men see her like that now.

"I opened it for us, my love." and Jennie smiles at her husband again in an attitude that is completely foreign to me.

"Come on, get the toy ." Frank orders impatiently. "You're welcome, my darling." Angie gets up and disappears into the room that was previously closed as a study.

Frank now turns to Angie. "So tell me, how did Jennie get you?" Frank's still ice-cold eyes flicker from hers to mine. "Yes, darling, I would be interested in that too."

Jennifer comes back into the room with a large sports bag, places it on the floor to the right of Frank and stands at attention again.

Angie gets up from the sofa and sits on my lap for protection, takes me in her arms and plays with my cock a little.

"We both did it occasionally when we were still at school," she says. "Frank and I don't want to hear that you dyed each other's hair."

I also took a little initiative.

"Jennie just licked my pussy like she used to,"

she smiles happily at Jennie. "Then she really pushed her hand into me, you know how much I like to be completely filled, and then I had to promise her that Frank would be allowed to fuck me." Now she was a little unsure again.

I pull the chain between her teats until she grimaces. "Aha," I say, "you always said to me that you could never imagine fucking with other people the way I want." "But darling, that's Jennie and I have that "Yeah, never thought of it and if it did," she reflected, "then with her and Frank."

Now at least that was clarified.

Frank now grabbed Jennifer's cheeks hard with one hand. "Didn't you make it clear to her how she was going to be fucked tonight!" "Yes, Frank, she knows exactly what she's doing.

" He pushes her head back.

Tell me!

he shouts at Angie.

"No," says Angie.

Frank's eyes shift to Jennie. "So you call that clarifying something?

"Go on, clear the table and if Angie isn't completely drunk, she'd better help you." I also wanted to help the two women quickly, my cock needed a warm sheath into which it could dip. "Hey, Harald are you completely stupid now?

Come on, give me a hand."

While the women tidy things up naked in the living room, Frank opens the sports bag.

The two women are a delightful sight, especially because my darling still has the chain dangling from her udders and it was clear that I would buy one of these for her when she got home.

Frank hands me two ropes with Velcro cuffs attached to the end. "For the feet," he said and begins to attach the counterparts for the hands to the table legs.

Angie pauses for a moment and looks at what we are doing. Some gravy runs from the plate onto her slightly domed stomach. Jennie licks the cold gravy before it drips onto the carpet. Surprised and then smiling again, the two women look at each other and continue their work.

A few steps between the living room and the kitchen later everything is done and Frank orders Jennie to lie down on the table.

Jennie quickly sat down on the table and stretched herself out.

Angie and I sit on a chair and position ourselves so that we can easily watch the game. Frank throws me a black cloth. "Come on, do something and blindfold your wife.

" It's okay. Angie nods lustfully and lets me blindfold her .

Frank carefully and calmly straps his wife onto the table. He checks the fit of the cuffs, strokes Jennifer's gap every now and then or pats her cheeks. When she is fixed, he goes around the table again, probably to check whether there is enough space on all sides.

"Now let's see how well Angie can lick. You don't mind, Harald?"

I shake my head. Frank takes Angie by the hand and blindly directs her between her friend's legs. Angie is a bit stubborn, but Frank gets rid of it with two not-too-severe blows on her buttocks. "Go ahead, lick the clit.

Always follow your nose with your nose," grins Frank.

I jerk my cock a little, by the way, just for my well-being. I've also switched back to beer. The cognac is a bit too strong after a while.

Angie kneels on the laminate, her knees slightly spread between Jennifer's thighs and begins to lick her pussy extensively while blindfolded. When she tries to use her hands to help, the whip "Snap" whizzes onto her left paw. "You're doing that again!" shouts Frank.

She jumps up as if frightened. It is unavoidable that the whip, even more than Angie's hand, hits Jenni's thigh and she immediately twitches violently because of the pain on the inside of her left thigh.

"She's doing well. Now let's see if we can find out what your little wife whore promised my wife. Jennie!" The tied woman immediately looked him in the eyes.

"And you keep licking,"

he orders Angie and she does so with a nice smack. "Come over here, Harald, and don't sit there doing nothing.

Play with your old woman's cunt, I don't care." I stand up and squat down behind my kneeling wife. I reach up to her crack from behind and share the hole. Nice and soft and wet. Didn't think she would like the game.

"Jennie! Did she tell you what I can have today?" The whip, slightly beaten, rushes down on her stomach and hits the flesh. I press Angie's head between Jennie's thighs. She wouldn't have been able to see anything anyway.

Jennie sucks in her breath. "She said it, Frank, honestly" "But now she won't say it and he struck again with the whip and Jennie squeals, her arms pull on the handcuffs and her hands claw at nothing.

The slap was harder, but Jennifer enjoys being spanked. My wife's tongue does the rest.

"It was an 11-letter word, right?" Another sudden bang and the girl squirms again. I have to admit, it looks really hot and I almost forget to take care of my wife's pussy.

"Okay, Angie. Even if you can't see anything at the moment, which I don't think is really important, I can at least tell you that it's your fault if Jennie has to suffer a little now. Or Jennie? She really said it. You're not lying to me, are you?

The whip cracks again, but this time with full force across Jennie's right breast. The bang makes her jump, that's real fear.

I can see it in her eyes, which were wide with shock. She must trust Frank a lot. It wobbles for a moment and then falls back to its original position.

Angie doesn't notice anything. I give her the three. Simply means middle finger in the ass and index and ring fingers in the pussy.

Wow, things are starting to get crazy. Otherwise it's a game between us that she says how many fingers she wants. Tonight I think it's inappropriate. Pussies have no say here and a cunt is just what it is.

Frank gradually placed twelve clamps on Jenni's stomach, whereupon her chest began to rise and fall violently. Nice picture actually. "11 is such an inappropriate number.

We'll just put one on top as a hyphen. Six for each breast, three for each syllable, right, my darling?" he grins again, his always disgusting grin.

"Please, not the little ones, take the big ones."

Jennie still seems to have a will of her own. Frank grabs Angie by the neck again.

"Aren't you going to save Jennie this and tell me what you want tonight? Sitting upright,

I had Angie comfortably on my paw and my fingers had easy play in the funnel.

Her hips show, her beautiful plump ass begins to rotate.

"Apparently your little one is mute. Well. Harald gives her a little doggy style while she slobbers her pussy on the table decorations. "You're my sweet little table decoration?" and his hands fall over Jennie's nipples and stretch them. Another picture in my head. Jennie bends in her bonds, tugs at the ropes, a poor, helpless thing.

Does she really enjoy it? You can also make Angie squirt if you touch her teats properly. But so violent? "Finally fuck your pig!" he shouts at me.

I position Angie , her buxom ass in front of my cock. I can't resist hitting it hard, which she responds to with a "mmmh". She's still licking Jennifer's clam.

That my wife would do something like that! I still can't believe my eyes. And doggy style too, I usually squirt very quickly, so I cover her slowly, very slowly.

Frank puts a tube of Flutschi within my reach. He nods at me as if asking me to prepare her rump. That's how it is.

My middle finger has already poked her flesh. But Angie's rosette is unruly . I let it run in slowly and with the first drops I have to hold Angie's hips and increase my thrusts. At this rate, at the sight of this, I would come in seconds. So get out with your tail and try out the four.

Her pussy is slippery enough. The lubricant is actually a waste. My fingers are comfortable, my thumb is rubbing Angie's clit.

My left hand had all the time in the world for her stubborn ass, which she doesn't take away from me either.

"So my sweet Jennie. We now do the following. I take these small, admittedly somewhat nasty brackets and you tell me the letter that corresponds to each bracket.

"Are we doing it like this?"

Frank plays with the brackets. Jennifer just enjoys my wife's tongue driving her to her first orgasm. She's standing very close to the edge. Angie has been licking her for at least ten minutes. "Let's do it like this!" and he turns her right nipple into a triple Axel.

"Yes,"

Jenni hisses.

"Yes, what!" followed by a double toe loop. "I say it, lover. "I'll tell you the letters," it pumps out of the abused chest. "Thanks sweetie. Understanding comes from learning and unfortunately women only learn through education ."

"Yes, Frank, educate me, touch me, make me whole."

Jennie twitches in her bonds.

"You don't have to repeat everything we learned together." He smiles and strokes her hair.

As if goaded, I drive Angie to orgasm with my right hand. I can't imagine that this will be her second fisting or let's say semi-fisting since the thumb is still missing.

Anticipation is raining out of my cock in thick threads. At that moment I wasn't even in the mood for Jennie's unknown field to order. My own mare already excites me enough.

"So, let's start number one up here."

"A" hisses out of Jennie's mouth.

The clamps are equipped with teeth and even though Frank leaves out her nipples, these things still pinch deep into the flesh of these rather pathetic boobs.

So, my wife has tits, but Jennie's milk dish is pug at best. "R, S,C,H" and the sixth bracket for the hyphen formed a beautiful wreath around the left breast.

Frank plays with the clips and Jenni fidgets. It's hard to say whether Jennie's tongue or the clamps are causing her to fidget. Jennifer could say stop, but that word is probably missing from her vocabulary.

Frank carries on and Jennie accepts everything. Something so cool.

"I'm coming, it's no longer possible...aaaaaaah."

And so Jennie runs out in front of my eyes, all of a sudden and actually without warning.

Angie is visibly relieved and immediately stops licking. "Assfucking" is all my wife says and is pretty out of breath.

Jennie's pussy juice has spread all around her mouth and far below her chin.

Frank looks at me and I don't. A condom goes over his hard-on. Like mine, it was just a cock.

Not big, not small, enough. "Come on, you bastard, pull me over the edge."

I didn't think I heard what Angie said. "You want to fuck ass, you sadist pig, then fuck your ass!"

Frank starts and gives Angie nothing. His hard-on makes its way. The entrance is narrow but he squeezes in.

I see Angie's stomach bulge and tense. It's not her first assfuck, not by a long shot, but this time there seems to be no limit, especially no pain.

Jennie lies there as if abandoned. I jump up and loosen the bonds, biting everything that comes to my face.

I bite her thighs, her slightly fatty hips, grab her tits, pull on the teats and loosen the clamps, I'm an idiot, Jennie cries out.

"Take a condom, you goat," it roared from my wife's ass. "Hit me, go hit me, you asshole," Frank doesn't need to be told twice.

The bag is not far away. He takes something that looks like a simple strap, but has a serpentine section at the front. "You'll get to know the asshole , maid of honor.

" And he starts smacking her with the dog whip, his dog in heat, his dog going out, which I actually didn't allow to go outside.

With every thrust he trims her bottom, disfigures it, makes it his own, marks the flesh with his name. Angie gasps a lot and utters wonderful, sometimes almost funny curses and curses.

Where is my board anyway? Still lying in front of me with her hands tied , I climb on the table and force my cock into her mouth.

"Fuck her tonsils properly,"

I hear it clapping from behind. He's using Angie that I don't even want to see, or does he?

I used Jennie in a way I could hardly imagine, now loosening her handcuffs while my cock oils the back of her throat and then, just as her hands were free, she actually bit me on the glans, the stupid bitch.

Go for the ass, she begs, kneeling right in front of Angie and looking for her hands.

Her buttocks stick up, round and sore. It wobbles wonderfully, you really don't see something like that often.

I use lubricant and oil the bearing. Then I drive into the shaft.

Jennie takes off Angie's blindfold. Grab it with both hands. "Your husband is fucking me in the ass, snail!" grunts Jennie.

"Mine just fucks you? Your brutal sack is blowing me open. Oh God, I can't take it anymore."

Frank is currently pushing a small vibrator under her clit.

"Do it yourself, woman."

and Angie grabs the piece of rubber and rolls to orgasm. I squirted first.

"Yes, inseminate me, take a good look at the maid of honor!

From today on you'll fuck me as a greeting!" Nothing can hold me up anymore and Jennie had also collapsed. I pump her full and just lower myself onto her.

My weight pushes her down. Her flapping breasts slapped the laminate.

Angie is far from having her pussy full and is ready to really get fucked. She's sexy, really fuckable and can be pounded in the ass.

But Frank doesn't have much to offer anymore. Two or three final thrusts, his hands cling to my wife's ready hips and then it's over. He unloads himself with a long grunt.

Jennie pulls the clamps from Angie's teats. It's coming to her. She screams, she moans, she lets herself go. "You perverted pigs, fuck me, fuck me, fuck me!" Then it's enough.

My sweetie lets the vibrator coast down and collapses.

The cock pops out of her violated and permanently dilated anus.

We men crawl up to our wives, caress and caress them. Frank goes into the kitchen and gives Jenni a drink.

She snuggles up to him. I grab a beer and toast everyone. It's time for bed. After all, there is a tomorrow and what a tomorrow.

www.ingramcontent.com/pod-product-compliance
Lightning Source LLC
Chambersburg PA
CBHW052236150726
48002CB00003B/1454